Laila's Wedding

by Kaleel Sakakeeny

Illustrated by
Helen Zughaib Shoreman

MULTICULTURAL CELEBRATIONS II

MODERN CURRICULUM PRESS

Multicultural Celebrations was created under the auspices of
 The Children's Museum, Boston.
Leslie Swartz, Director of Teacher Services,
directed this project.

We would like to thank Amal Arnaout,
Carole Courey, Nazik Kazimi and Hayat Shalhoub
for their contributions to this story.

Design: Gary Fujiwara
Photographs: *5, 12, 18*, Wendie Sakakeeny.

 MODERN CURRICULUM PRESS, INC.
13900 Prospect Road
Cleveland, Ohio 44136

ISBN 0-8136-2327-8 (soft cover)   0-8136-2328-6 (hard cover)

2 3 4 5 6 7 8 9 10   98 97 96 95 94

Simon & Schuster   A Paramount Communications Company

The Karem house was glowing with excitement.
Everything was ready for the wedding tomorrow.
The smell of wonderful foods filled the air. Furniture
had been moved to make way for the dancing.
Relatives poured into the house. The Karems gladly
welcomed everyone.

1

"When will the plane from Lebanon land in New York?" Amal asked her mother as they finished the food for tonight's party.

"Uncle Hassan and Aunt Samira will be here soon," Mrs. Karem answered. "You're so excited someone might think you're the bride and not your sister. You know, they're bringing a special gift for Laila."

"A special gift?" Amal wondered. This was Amal's first family wedding.

"Here, taste this," her mother said. The *fatayer,* rolled grape leaves, and the *tabooli* salad were delicious. But a date and nut-filled pastry called *maamool* was Amal's favorite.

Suddenly, Uncle Hassan and Aunt Samira burst through the door carrying packages. Laughter, tears, and hugs mixed as everyone wished them *"Ahalan Wa Sahalan,"* Arabic for welcome.

"Now for the best part!" Uncle Hassan announced. "We have brought gifts for everyone."

For Amal's mother, there was a jewelry box of Lebanese cedar wood. Ziad, her brother, received a *dirrabaki* to play for the dancers. And for Amal there was a doll in traditional Arab clothing.

"Yours must be next, Laila — your special gift," Amal said.

But Aunt Samira suddenly gasped, "It's not here — oh no — the gift for Laila! The box is not here..."

"How is that possible?" asked Uncle Hassan. "We carried the gift with the others."

"It was a small box wrapped in gold paper. We must find it." Aunt Samira said.

"Amal will help you search. She has a knack for finding lost things," Mrs. Karem offered.

"Don't worry. We'll find it—*Inshallah*—God willing" said Amal's father. "Now, let's eat. We have a wedding to celebrate."

Later, the special gift still had not been found. Even Amal, who prided herself on finding lost objects, had no luck.

6

The next morning Amal helped her sister into the beautiful white gown. Then her mother gave Laila a *bighji* colorful, gold-threaded silk cloth for wrapping and carrying personal things.

"This *bighji* has been handed down from mother to daughter for generations," she said. "*Bil hanna.* Enjoy it in happiness."

"I hear the *zalghoota*," Laila laughed. There on the lawn were her women friends and relatives. They were making a happy, trilling sound to wish her luck.

"Of course. This is a very special occasion," her mother said.

9

At the *mosque* the *Imam* and his wife greeted the
family.

"Who are the chairs for?" Amal asked her mother.

"Two chairs are for Laila and Omar, two are for
their fathers, and two more are for the witnesses.
The rest of us will sit back here."

The *Imam* read the first verse from the *Koran,* the
Muslim holy book. Amal listened as he asked Omar
and Laila if they agreed to be husband and wife.

"Yes," they answered loudly. Everyone laughed.

Omar and Laila gave each other rings and kissed.
The short ceremony ended and the family rushed up
to congratulate them.

11

When Laila entered the hotel for the wedding reception the *zalghoota* began again. Then the *zaffee*, a swirl of musicians and dancers, led everyone into the room. The guests applauded.

Friends and family joined the traditional *dabki*, dancing in and out around the tables in a long line. Everyone shared the delicious food.

Uncle Hassan and Aunt Samira wore the only sad faces. Their gift was still missing.

"Wait," said Uncle Hassan. "We almost forgot the *mulabbas*. Amal and Ziad, can you get them out of the car?"

"*Mulabbas?*" Amal asked.

"Jordan almonds — traditional gifts given to each wedding guest. "

At the car, Amal climbed into the back seat. "Ziad, I'll hand you boxes," she said and stopped. "What's this?" Something glittered on the floor.

"Ziad, look— a box wrapped in gold paper! It must be the special gift... I knew I would find it!" she cried.

Amal and Ziad rushed back to the wedding party.

"Amal... that's it! You've found Laila's gift!" Aunt Samira cried with relief.

"Oh, how beautiful," Laila said as she opened the box.

"Laila, this necklace was made in Syria," explained Uncle Hassan. "In ancient times, craftspeople there made gold jewelry and steel swords. We have brought you this Arab treasure on your wedding day. It is a part of your heritage you can keep forever."

18

Laila and Amal could see their faces in the shiny gold.

"And this treasure will pass to my daughter, when she marries, and to her daughter in time," Laila said.

"Well, we had better keep it in a place where we can find it!" Amal said laughing.

"*Inshallah*," said Mr. and Mrs. Karem. "From generation to generation."

20

Glossary

dabki (DAB-keh) the traditional Arab line dance

dirrabaki (dur-ah-BAHK-ee) a drum with a round top and narrow base

fatayer (fah-TIE-yeh) a pastry filled with meat or spinach

Imam (ee-MAHM) a leader in the Muslim religion

Koran (qu-RAHN) the Holy Book of Islam

maamool (mah-MOOL) a sweet pastry filled with nuts and dates

mosque (MAHSK) a Muslim place of worship

mulabbas (moo-LAH-bahs) almonds grown in Jordan that are given as gifts

tabooli (tah-BOO-leh) a salad made of wheat, parsley and other seasonings

zaffee (ZAHF-fee) a parade of musicians and dancers that lead a bride and groom

zalghoota (zahl-GHOO-tah) a trilling sound that Arab women make to show happiness

About the Author

Kaleel Sakakeeny is an Arab American whose family comes from Syria. For many years he has been a broadcast and print journalist. He has always been interested in other cultures and does much of his reporting about developing parts of the world. When he is not traveling on assignment, he lives in Boston, Massachusetts with his wife and two daughters.

About the Illustrator

Helen Zughaib Shoreman was born in Beirut, Lebanon. She has lived and traveled all over the Middle East and Europe. In 1977, she came to New York to study art at Syracuse University. She now lives in Washington, D.C. with her husband, Michael, and her two cats, Noodle and Chunky Beef.